The Pirate Pie Ship

by Adam and Charlotte Guillain

Illustrated by Rupert Van Wyk

Crabtree Publishing Company

www.crabtreebooks.com

Crabtree Publishing Company
www.crabtreebooks.com
1-800-387-7650

616 Welland Ave.   PMB 59051, 350 Fifth Ave.
St. Catharines, ON   59th Floor,
L2M 5V6   New York, NY 10118

Published by Crabtree Publishing Company in 2015

First published in 2012 by Franklin Watts
(A division of Hachette Children's Books)

Text © Adam and Charlotte Guillain 2012
Illustration © Rupert Van Wyk 2012

Series editor: Melanie Palmer
Series advisor: Catherine Glavina
Series designer: Peter Scoulding
Editor: Kathy Middleton
Proofreader and
    notes to adults: Shannon Welbourn
Production coordinator and
    Prepress technician: Katherine Berti
Print coordinator: Katherine Berti

Printed in Hong Kong/082014/BK20140613

Library and Archives Canada Cataloguing in Publication

Cuillain, Adam, author
    The pirate pie ship / by Adam and Charlotte Cuillain ; illustrated by Rupert Van Wyk.

(Race ahead with reading)
Issued in print and electronic formats.
ISBN 978-0-7787-1309-8 (bound).--
ISBN 978-0-7787-1368-5 (pbk.).--
ISBN 978-1-4271-7784-1 (pdf).--
ISBN 978-1-4271-7772-8 (html)

        I. Cuillain, Charlotte, author II. Van Wyk, Rupert, illustrator III. Title.

PZ7.C96Pi 2014   j823'.92   C2014-903706-6
                                      C2014-903707-4

Library of Congress Cataloging-in-Publication Data

Guillain, Adam, author.
    The pirate pie ship / by Adam Guillain and Charlotte Guillain ; illustrated by Rupert Van Wyk.
        pages cm. -- (Race ahead with reading)
    "First published in 2012 by Franklin Watts"--Copyright page.
    ISBN 978-0-7787-1309-8 (reinforced library binding) -- ISBN 978-0-7787-1368-5 (pbk.) -- ISBN 978-1-4271-7784-1 (electronic pdf) -- ISBN 978-1-4271-7772-8 (electronic html)
    [1. Pirates--Fiction. 2. Pies--Fiction.] I. Guillain, Charlotte, author. II. Van Wyk, Rupert, illustrator. III. Title.

PZ7.G93847Pi 2014
[E]--dc23
                            2014020702

Chapter 1

The Planktown Pirates were tired. They were tired of scaring sailors. They were tired of chasing other ships. They were tired of digging for treasure.

And most of all, they were tired of fighting their pirate rivals, the Gruesome Crew.

"I feel like trying something new," sighed Captain Cuttlefish.

"But what?" asked Manta Ray Jack, the ship's first mate.

"Being pirates is all we know," moaned Connor the cabin boy.

Cook Cockles watched the crew slump in despair. He decided to cook the captain's favorite dish—octopus and seaweed pie— for lunch.

"This pie will help you think of ideas," said Cook Cockles. He served up a steaming slice of pie for the captain.

Captain Cuttlefish ate a mouthful of pie. Then he ate another. A twinkle came into his eye as he looked around at the crew gobbling down their lunch.

"That's it!" he cried. The crew looked up,
but they didn't stop eating.

"Your delicious pies are the
finest on the seven seas,"
the captain told Cook Cockles.
"We can sell them in the port
and make a fortune!"

The crew cheered and raised their
mugs of lemonade.

"Here's to the Planktown Pirates' Pie Ship!"
bellowed Captain Cuttlefish.

"Now, let's get making pies!"

8

Chapter 2

For the rest of the day, the pirates worked hard catching fish. In the galley, Cook Cockles turned the whole crew into chefs in training.

They chopped and scraped...

and stirred...

and baked.

Soon the first batch of pies was ready.

"Set sail for the port!" shouted the Captain.

"Full speed ahead!"

The crew leaped into action.

Connor the cabin boy had painted *Pirate Pie Ship* in big letters on the largest sail. The skull and crossbones had been taken down, and a new flag was flying in its place.

As the ship sailed into the port, a large group of hungry sailors was waiting. The smell of delicious pies wafted over the port. The sailors raced over and jostled into a line.

"Today's specials are anchovy and
algae pie, and sardine and seagrass pie,"
shouted Manta Ray Jack.
"Come and get it! Only three gold coins
for a pie!"

13

Soon the pirates had sold every single pie. The sailors were begging them to come back the next day. Captain Cuttlefish sat on the deck and counted the coins.

"This beats digging for treasure! We'll be rich soon!" the crew cheered.

None of the pirates noticed the Gruesome

Crew's ship sailing silently into the port.

And nobody noticed they were being

watched through a spyglass.

Chapter 3

The next morning the happy pirates got to work making more pies.

At midday they set sail for the port again. They could see another line of starving sailors waiting for them.

But as they got closer, another ship suddenly appeared from behind the cliff and sailed quickly up to the hungry sailors.

"My spyglass! Now!" shouted Captain Cuttlefish. He held it to his eye and stared at the other ship.

"Curses and barnacles!" he roared.
"It's the Gruesome Crew! Their ship
has always been faster than ours."

Captain Cuttlefish looked more closely. He
could see *The Gruesome Fish and Chip Ship*
painted on the side of their enemy's ship.

The Gruesome Crew was laughing as they served up huge plates of fish and chips to the line of eager customers. Their leader, Captain Sharkfin, was counting piles and piles of gold and silver coins.

"Sail faster!" shouted
Captain Cuttlefish.

But by the time the Planktown Pirates
reached the port, all the sailors had
licked their plates clean and disappeared.
There wasn't a single customer left.

"This means war!" Captain Cuttlefish shouted at the Gruesome Crew, as their ships drew alongside each other.

"You'll never win!" sneered Captain Sharkfin, with an evil laugh.

Chapter 4

The next morning the pirates got to work

again catching fish and making pies.

Connor the cabin boy jumped into

a rowboat and set off for the port.

When he arrived, he put out a sign saying "Mullet and Kelp Pie." He stood beside it holding a large, empty basket. The hungry sailors saw Connor's sign but were disappointed that he had no pies to sell.

"Your pies are the most delicious food around," said one sailor.

"And the Gruesome Crew isn't very friendly," agreed another. "But we're always so hungry by lunchtime, we'll eat their fish and chips if they get here first."

And sure enough, at midday the Gruesome

Crew's ship sailed swiftly into the port.

The smell of chips blew in on the wind,

and the sailors started to line up.

Chapter 5

"Wait!" shouted Connor, waving a flag.

BOOM!

The sailors all turned to see what

the noise was.

BOOM!

Out at sea, the Planktown Pirates' ship was firing its cannons right at the port!

BOOM!

BOOM!

Connor held up his basket and started to catch the piping hot pies being fired from the ship. They smelled delicious!

The sailors gasped and turned back to Connor, who happily handed out pies and took gold coins.

The Gruesome Crew could only watch as
all the sailors munched on the hot pies.
Then they looked up.

The pies had shot right through their
ship's sails. They were in tatters!
The Gruesome Crew wouldn't be sailing
anywhere for a while.

As the sailors munched the last
of their pies, the Planktown Pirates
sailed into the port cheering.

Captain Cuttlefish was holding up another huge pie.

"Chocolate and cherry pie for everyone!" he shouted.

And all the sailors jumped aboard for dessert.

Notes for Adults

These entertaining, first chapter books help children build up their reading skills so they can move on to longer books. Fun illustrations and bite-sized chapters encourage young readers to take the driver's seat and *Race Ahead with Reading*.

THE FOLLOWING BEFORE, DURING, AND AFTER READING ACTIVITY SUGGESTIONS SUPPORT LITERACY SKILL DEVELOPMENT AND CAN ENRICH SHARED READING EXPERIENCES:

BEFORE

1. Make reading fun! Choose a time to read when you and the reader are relaxed and have time to share the story together. Don't forget to give praise! Children learn best in a positive environment.
2. Before reading, ask the reader to look at the title and illustration on the cover of the book **The Pirate Pie Ship**. Invite them to make predictions about what will happen in the story. They may make use of prior knowledge and make connections to other stories they have heard or read about pirates or similar characters.

DURING

3. Encourage readers to determine unfamiliar words themselves by using clues from the text and illustrations.
4. During reading, encourage the child to review his or her understanding and see if they want to revise their predictions midway. Encourage the reader to make text-to-text connections, choosing a part of the story that reminds them of another story they have read; and text-to-self connections, choosing a part of the story that relates to their own personal experiences; and text-to-world connections, choosing a part of the story that reminds them of something that happened in the real world.

AFTER

5. Ask the reader who the main characters are in this story. Have the child retell the story in their own words. Ask him or her to think about the predictions they made before reading the story. How were they the same or different?

DISCUSSION QUESTIONS FOR KIDS

6. Throughout this story, the Planktown Pirates are presented with problems. How do they solve the problems they face?
7. Choose one of the illustrations from the story. How do the details in the picture help you understand a part of the story better? Or, what do they tell you that is not in the text?
8. Which character in this story do you relate to most? Explain why.
9. How does the Gruesome Crew interfere with the Planktown Pirates' new pie business?
10. What moral, or lesson, can you take from this story?
11. Create your own story or drawing about a time when you worked together with someone to solve a problem.